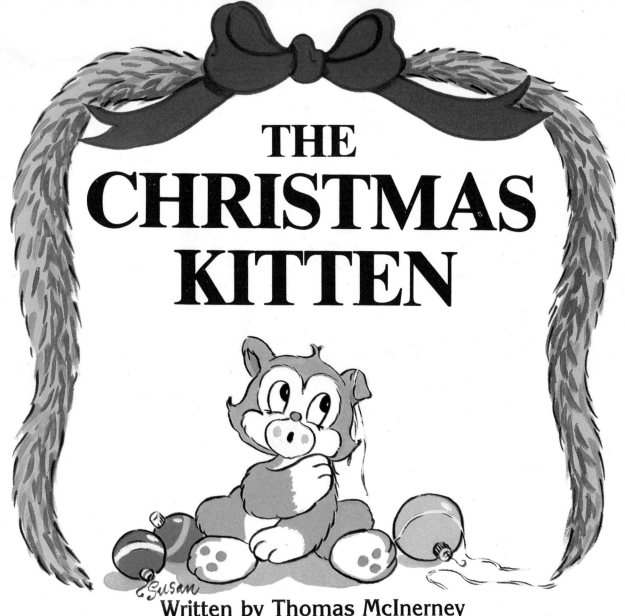

THE
CHRISTMAS
KITTEN

Written by Thomas McInerney
Illustrated by Susan Marino

Modern Publishing
A Division of Unisystems, Inc.
New York, New York 10022

On Christmas Eve, for the first time ever, Tommy and Karin were decorating the tree. Their new kitten, Tiger, was helping—well, sort of!

"No, no, Tiger," said Karin, as the frisky kitten swung at a tree ornament. Tommy caught it before it fell. Tiger jumped out of Karin's arms.

He scooted under the tree and crawled into an empty box.
The twins hung their stockings over the fireplace.
"Do you think Santa's nearby?" asked Karin.
"Let's look," said Tommy.

The twins looked up the chimney chute. All they could see were stars way up in the sky.

"Well, well! You two did a wonderful job decorating the tree!" laughed their father behind them.

"Tiger helped too, Dad," said Tommy.

"You'd better get to bed now or Santa won't come," Dad said.

"Wait! Where's Tiger?" said Karin, looking around.

"He's probably just playing. He'll come upstairs soon," said Dad. And he carried Karin and Tommy up to bed.

Downstairs, Tiger was ready for adventure!
The kitten scampered in between the papers and boxes.
He chased a rolling Christmas ball around the room. It
rolled right to the edge of the fireplace.

Tiger looked up the chimney chute. Stars twinkled above. The curious kitten climbed up the chimney. Soon he was halfway up—and the floor looked very far away! How would Tiger get back down?

There was a loud noise on the roof. Tiger looked up and saw a man dressed in a red suit. He had a great big sack and he was climbing down the chimney!

"Meow! Meow!" cried Tiger.

"Well, well!" chuckled Santa when he saw the kitten. "Don't worry, little fellow. I'll help you."

Santa scooped Tiger up and placed him on top of the presents in his sack.

"Ho! Ho Ho!" laughed Santa, as Tiger rolled out from the sack. As Santa pulled out presents, Tiger untied ribbons and ripped open packages. Santa chased after the kitten.

"You're a lively little fellow!" smiled Santa. Then he put Tiger into one of the pockets of his big red coat. Tiger peeked out while Santa finished his work.

Soon it was time for Santa's snack.

"Here, little kitten," Santa said, and shared the milk with Tiger. Santa laughed and laughed as the kitten tried to wipe the drops of milk off his whiskers.

"You certainly made a mess!" chuckled Santa.

Santa was ready to leave. He had many other stops to make before morning and he couldn't stay to keep Tiger out of trouble. Santa looked at Tiger and smiled.

"I know what I'll do with you!"

When Tommy and Karin woke up, they couldn't find Tiger anywhere. They ran downstairs to look for him, but stopped when they saw the Christmas tree.

"Look at that present, Tommy! What could it be?" Karin pointed to an oddly wrapped box with holes poked in it and a big red bow on top. The box seemed to be wiggling!

Tommy opened the lid. Out jumped Tiger!

The twins laughed and agreed that Tiger was the best Christmas present ever.

"But how did he get into that box?" they wondered. Tiger purred. That was a secret between him and Santa!